# FARMER IN THE DELL

Retold by STEVEN ANDERSON

Illustrated by MAXINE LEE

CANTATA
LEARNING

MANKATO, MINNESOTA

WWW.CANTATALEARNING.COM

CANTATA
LEARNING
MANKATO, MINNESOTA

Published by Cantata Learning
1710 Roe Crest Drive
North Mankato, MN 56003
www.cantatalearning.com

Library of Congress Control Number: 2014957019
978-1-63290-289-4 (hardcover/CD)
978-1-63290-441-6 (paperback/CD)
978-1-63290-483-6 (paperback)

*Farmer in the Dell* by Steven Anderson
Illustrated by Maxine Lee

Book design, Tim Palin Creative
Editorial direction, Flat Sole Studio
Executive musical production and direction, Elizabeth Draper
Music arranged and produced by Steven C Music

Printed in the United States of America.

VISIT
**WWW.CANTATALEARNING.COM/ACCESS-OUR-MUSIC**
TO SING ALONG TO THE SONG

The farmer and his family are having a party!

There will be music and dancing. It's a **hoedown**!

Should we see who comes to the party?

Now turn the page, and sing along.

4

The farmer in the **dell**.

The farmer in the dell.

**Heigh-ho** the derry-o,

The farmer in the dell!

The farmer takes a wife.

The farmer takes a wife.

Heigh-ho the derry-o,

The farmer takes a wife!

The wife takes the child.
The wife takes the child.

Heigh-ho the derry-o,
The wife takes the child!

The child takes the dog.
The child takes the dog.

Heigh-ho the derry-o,
The child takes the dog!

The dog takes the cat.

The dog takes the cat

Heigh-ho the derry-o,

The dog takes the cat!

The cat takes a mouse.

The cat takes a mouse.

Heigh-ho the derry-o,

The cat takes a mouse!

The mouse takes the cheese.

The mouse takes the cheese.

Heigh-ho the derry-o,

The mouse takes the cheese!

The cheese stands alone.

The cheese stands alone.

Heigh-ho the derry-o,

The cheese stands alone!

Heigh-ho the derry-o,

The cheese stands alone!

# SONG LYRICS
## Farmer in the Dell

The farmer in the dell.
The farmer in the dell.

Heigh–ho the derry–o,
The farmer in the dell!

The farmer takes a wife.
The farmer takes a wife.
Heigh–ho the derry–o,
The farmer takes a wife!

The wife takes the child.
The wife takes the child.

Heigh–ho the derry–o,
The wife takes the child!

The child takes the dog.
The child takes the dog.

Heigh–ho the derry–o,
The child takes the dog!

The dog takes the cat.
The dog takes the cat.

Heigh–ho the derry–o,
The dog takes the cat!

The cat takes a mouse.
The cat takes a mouse.

Heigh–ho the derry–o,
The cat takes a mouse!

The mouse takes
   the cheese.
The mouse takes
   the cheese.

Heigh–ho the derry–o,
The mouse takes the
   cheese!

The cheese stands alone.
The cheese stands alone.

Heigh–ho the derry–o,
The cheese stands alone!

Heigh–ho the derry–o,
The cheese stands alone!

# Farmer in the Dell

**Americana**
Steven C Music

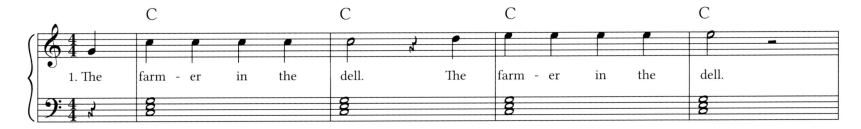

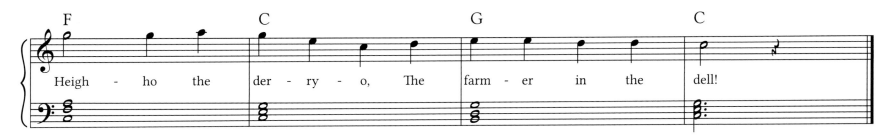

**Verse 2**
The farmer takes a wife.
The farmer takes a wife.

Heigh-ho the derry-o,
The farmer takes a wife!

**Verse 3**
The wife takes the child.
The wife takes the child.

Heigh-ho the derry-o,
The wife takes the child!

**Verse 4**
The child takes the dog.
The child takes the dog.

Heigh-ho the derry-o,
The child takes the dog!

**Verse 5**
The dog takes the cat.
The dog takes the cat.

Heigh-ho the derry-o,
The dog takes the cat!

**Verse 6**
The cat takes a mouse.
The cat takes a mouse.

Heigh-ho the derry-o,
The cat takes a mouse!

**Verse 7**
The mouse takes the cheese.
The mouse takes the cheese.

Heigh-ho the derry-o,
The mouse takes the cheese!

**Verse 8**
The cheese stands alone.
The cheese stands alone.

Heigh-ho the derry-o,
The cheese stands alone!

Heigh-ho the derry-o,
The cheese stands alone!

# GLOSSARY

**dell**—a small, low land area with trees and grass growing on it

**heigh-ho**—a saying used to show tiredness

**hoedown**—a country party with music and dancing

# GUIDED READING ACTIVITIES

1.  Who is the illustrator of this book? What does an illustrator do?

2.  List all of the characters, people, and animals, in this story. Who did each of them dance with?

3.  Add another character to the story. Draw your character dancing with one of the characters in this book.

## TO LEARN MORE

Close, Laura Ferraro. *The Farmer in the Dell*. Mankato, MN: Child's World, 2011.

Diaz, Joanne Ruelos. *Animals on the Farm*. Minneapolis, MN: Picture Window Books, 2015.

Dickmann, Nancy. *Farm Animals*. Chicago, IL: Heinemann-Raintree, 2011.

Ready, Dee. *Farmers Help*. North Mankato, MN: Capstone Press, 2014.